GAULISH VILLAGE

COMPENDIUM

LAUDANUM

AQUARIUM

TOTORUM

ARMORICA

BELGICA

LUTETIA

SPQR

GAUL
(ROMAN CONQUEST)
50 BC

CELTICA

AQUITANIA

PROVINCIA

THE YEAR IS 50 BC. GAUL IS ENTIRELY OCCUPIED BY THE
ROMANS. WELL, NOT ENTIRELY ... ONE SMALL VILLAGE OF
INDOMITABLE GAULS STILL HOLDS OUT AGAINST THE INVADERS.
AND LIFE IS NOT EASY FOR THE ROMAN LEGIONARIES WHO
GARRISON THE FORTIFIED CAMPS OF TOTORUM, AQUARIUM,
LAUDANUM AND COMPENDIUM ...

ASTERIX, THE HERO OF THESE ADVENTURES. A SHREWD, CUNNING LITTLE WARRIOR, ALL PERILOUS MISSIONS ARE IMMEDIATELY ENTRUSTED TO HIM. ASTERIX GETS HIS SUPERHUMAN STRENGTH FROM THE MAGIC POTION BREWED BY THE DRUID GETAFIX . . .

OBELIX, ASTERIX'S INSEPARABLE FRIEND. A MENHIR DELIVERY MAN BY TRADE, ADDICTED TO WILD BOAR. OBELIX IS ALWAYS READY TO DROP EVERYTHING AND GO OFF ON A NEW ADVENTURE WITH ASTERIX – SO LONG AS THERE'S WILD BOAR TO EAT, AND PLENTY OF FIGHTING. HIS CONSTANT COMPANION IS DOGMATIX, THE ONLY KNOWN CANINE ECOLOGIST, WHO HOWLS WITH DESPAIR WHEN A TREE IS CUT DOWN.

GETAFIX, THE VENERABLE VILLAGE DRUID, GATHERS MISTLETOE AND BREWS MAGIC POTIONS. HIS SPECIALITY IS THE POTION WHICH GIVES THE DRINKER SUPERHUMAN STRENGTH. BUT GETAFIX ALSO HAS OTHER RECIPES UP HIS SLEEVE . . .

CACOFONIX, THE BARD. OPINION IS DIVIDED AS TO HIS MUSICAL GIFTS. CACOFONIX THINKS HE'S A GENIUS. EVERY-ONE ELSE THINKS HE'S UNSPEAKABLE. BUT SO LONG AS HE DOESN'T SPEAK, LET ALONE SING, EVERYBODY LIKES HIM . . .

FINALLY, VITALSTATISTIX, THE CHIEF OF THE TRIBE. MAJESTIC, BRAVE AND HOT-TEMPERED, THE OLD WARRIOR IS RESPECTED BY HIS MEN AND FEARED BY HIS ENEMIES. VITALSTATISTIX HIMSELF HAS ONLY ONE FEAR, HE IS AFRAID THE SKY MAY FALL ON HIS HEAD TOMORROW. BUT AS HE ALWAYS SAYS, TOMORROW NEVER COMES.

THE FIERCELY INDEPENDENT LITTLE VILLAGE WHERE ASTERIX AND THE OTHER GAULS LIVE IS AT PEACE...

GOOD HUNTING, ASTERIX?

NOTHING MUCH TODAY...

OBELIX IS HAPPILY AT WORK, CARVING OUT A MENHIR...

THERE'LL ALWAYS BE A GAU-AAUL...

CACOFONIX THE BARD IS GIVING THE CHILDREN LESSONS...

WELL, YOUNG MAN, AND INTO HOW MANY PARTS IS GAUL DIVIDED?

VIII × V = XL

$$\begin{array}{r} III \\ + I \\ \hline = IV \end{array}$$

?

IN SHORT, EVERYONE IS CONTENTED. ALL IS PEACE AND PLENTY...

ANOTHER BOAR, OBELIX?

YES, PLEASE!

WHEN SUDDENLY...

OH, BY TOUTATIS!

?? ? ? ?

7

NEXT MORNING...

Auf wiedersehen!

The Cont Barbaria

HEY, ASTERIX, WHY DO YOU THINK THAT TRAVELLER TOLD US SICKLES WERE IN SHORT SUPPLY IN LUTETIA?

NO IDEA, OBELIX.

LET'S ENJOY OUR JOURNEY; WE CAN WORRY ABOUT THAT LATER...

THE ROMANS ARE RUINING THE LANDSCAPE WITH ALL THESE MODERN BUILDINGS!

OUR FRIENDS' JOURNEY PROCEEDS WITHOUT MUCH INCIDENT, APART FROM A FEW SCUFFLES WITH BANDITS...

AT SUINDINUM, ASTERIX AND OBELIX ARE UNABLE TO FIND A BED, AS IT HAPPENS TO BE THE DAY OF THE GREAT OX-CART RACE, THE SUINDINUM 24 HOURS...

BUT AT LAST, ONE DAY...

LOOK! OBELIX!

LUTETIA!

ISN'T IT BIG!

AVE, O SURPLUS DAIRIPRODUS.

AVE, OLD CHAP, AVE...

WHO ARE THESE PEOPLE DISTURBING MY MEAL?

GAULS. SOME GAULS HAVE BEEN HAVING A PUNCH-UP.

I'M TIRED OF GAULS. THEY'RE ALWAYS FIGHTING. IT'S SUCH A BORE...

THESE TWO GAULS HAVE BROKEN UP NAVISHTRIX'S PLACE.

HAD A DROP TOO MUCH BEER, EH?

NO. WE WERE JUST TRYING TO BUY A GOLDEN SICKLE FOR OUR DRUID.

I ALWAYS THOUGHT NAVISHTRIX WAS MIXED UP IN THIS SICKLE-TRAFFICKING BUSINESS...

HOW VERY PERSPICACIOUS OF YOU, O SURPLUS DAIRIPRODUS.

ALL RIGHT, ALL RIGHT. RELEASE THESE GAULS, I FIND THEM TIRING... WHAT A BORE, WHAT A BORE...

WHAT IS ALL THIS ABOUT A SICKLE-TRAFFICKING BUSINESS?

OH, THERE'S A GANG OF GOLDEN-SICKLE-TRAFFICKERS IN LUTETIA. SICKLES ARE IN GREAT DEMAND, BECAUSE OF THE CONFERENCE IN THE FOREST OF THE CARNUTES...

WHAT DID HE MEAN, WHAT A BOAR? I CAN'T SEE ONE ANYWHERE...

SO NOW THEY HAVE THE MONOPOLY, ESPECIALLY AS METALLURGIX DISAPPEARED WITHOUT LEAVING ANY FORWARDING ADDRESS...

BUT THEN... PERHAPS THEY'VE KIDNAPPED METALLURGIX?

KIDNAPPED OR MURDERED... WELL, OFF YOU GO, AND I DON'T WANT TO SEE ANY MORE OF YOU!

BOOOHOOOO! POOR COUSIN METALLURGIX!

16

20

BOOOHOOOO! POOR COUSIN METALLURGIX!

WE'LL FIND HIM, OBELIX. FOR A START, WHAT DOES YOUR COUSIN LOOK LIKE?

WHAT DOES HE LOOK LIKE? I'VE NO IDEA. I'VE NEVER SET EYES ON HIM.

!

LET'S GO BACK TO HIS HOUSE. WE MIGHT FIND A CLUE THERE...

SO WE MIGHT. HOW CAN I BE EXPECTED TO KNOW WHAT HE LOOKS LIKE WHEN I'VE NEVER SEEN HIM....? SOMETIMES ASTERIX JUST DOESN'T STOP TO THINK!

THE DOOR'S LOCKED, OF COURSE...

LEAVE IT TO ME. I'LL OPEN IT...

CRAAASH!

THERE YOU ARE!

WHAT A MESS! THAT'S FUNNY; WE'RE RATHER TIDY IN MY FAMILY...

THERE'S BEEN A FIGHT HERE. LOOK, METALLURGIX HAS LEFT HIS PERSONAL BELONGINGS AND HIS KITCHEN UTENSILS BEHIND...

BUT HIS TOOLS, HIS SICKLES AND HIS MONEY ARE ALL MISSING. OBELIX, YOUR COUSIN'S BEEN KIDNAPPED BY THE SICKLE-TRAFFICKERS!

BOOHOOO! POOR METALLURGIX!

WELL, THIS PROVES METALLURGIX IS STILL ALIVE. WE'LL FIND HIM, BY TOUTATIS!

OH, GOODY!

LET'S MOVE IN HERE, AND FIRST, LET'S GO AND DO SOME SHOPPING.

GOOD IDEA!

LATER...

WHAT A PRICE BOAR IS IN LUTETIA!

AND THE BUTCHER SAID PRICES WERE GOING TO RISE EVEN HIGHER. IT'S A POOR LOOKOUT FOR GAUL!

17

21

THE SUN, RISING ON LUTETIA, IS GREETED BY A COCKEREL...

COCK-A-DOODLE-DO!

GET UP, OBELIX! IT'S TIME TO START OUR INVESTIGATIONS!

THAT'S RIGHT. WE MUST FIND METALLURGIX.

LET'S GO BACK TO THAT ARVERNIAN IN THE WINE SHOP. I'M SURE HE KNOWS SOMETHING!

THE SUN OF MASSILIA

OH!

COULD YOU TELL US WHERE TO FIND THE ARVERNIAN WHO...

OH, I EXPECT YOU MEAN THE FORMER PROPRIETOR?

THAT CRAZY GAUL WHO SOLD ME THIS PLACE FOR A HANDFUL OF BRONZE COINS! IT'S UNDER NEW MANAGEMENT NOW, BUT YOU WON'T BE DISAPPOINTED!

I CAN OFFER YOU MY SPECIALITY: FISH SOUP! MADE OF NICE FRESH FISH, JUST ARRIVED BY OX-CART FROM MASSILIA!

DO YOU KNOW WHERE THE ARVERNIAN HAS GONE?

OH! HE STARTED FOR GERGOVIA THIS MORNING, TRAVELLING BY OX-CART, THE SAME AS THE FISH!

THE SUN OF MASSILIA

WHAT A SHAME! IF YOU'D COME A LITTLE SOONER YOU'D HAVE FOUND HIM STILL HERE!

THANKS!

ALL THESE LUTETIANS ARE CRAZY, BY BELISAMA!

18

WARM RAYS OF BRILLIANT SUNSHINE LIGHT UP A CLOUDLESS SKY...

...LITTLE BIRDS WARBLE ON THE LEAFY BRANCHES...

...SQUIRRELS PLAY ON THE MOSSY GROUND.

...WHILE UNDERNEATH THE MOSSY GROUND...

BOING

PLAF!

OUCH!

EEEEH

GET THEM, OBELIX!

YOU BET I WILL, ASTERIX!

BOUM!

ARE THERE ANY LEFT, ASTERIX?

NO, OBELIX, YOU'RE JUST FINISHING OFF THE LAST ONE...

BONG! BONG! BONG!

LET'S GET OUT OF HERE AND WARN THE BOSS!

OBELIX, I'M A BIT WORRIED... I CAN'T FIND NAVISHTRIX!

HE CAN'T HAVE COME TO ANY HARM. HE WAS HERE JUST NOW!

ANYWAY, I'VE GOT CLOVOGARLIX.

THAT'S SOMETHING...

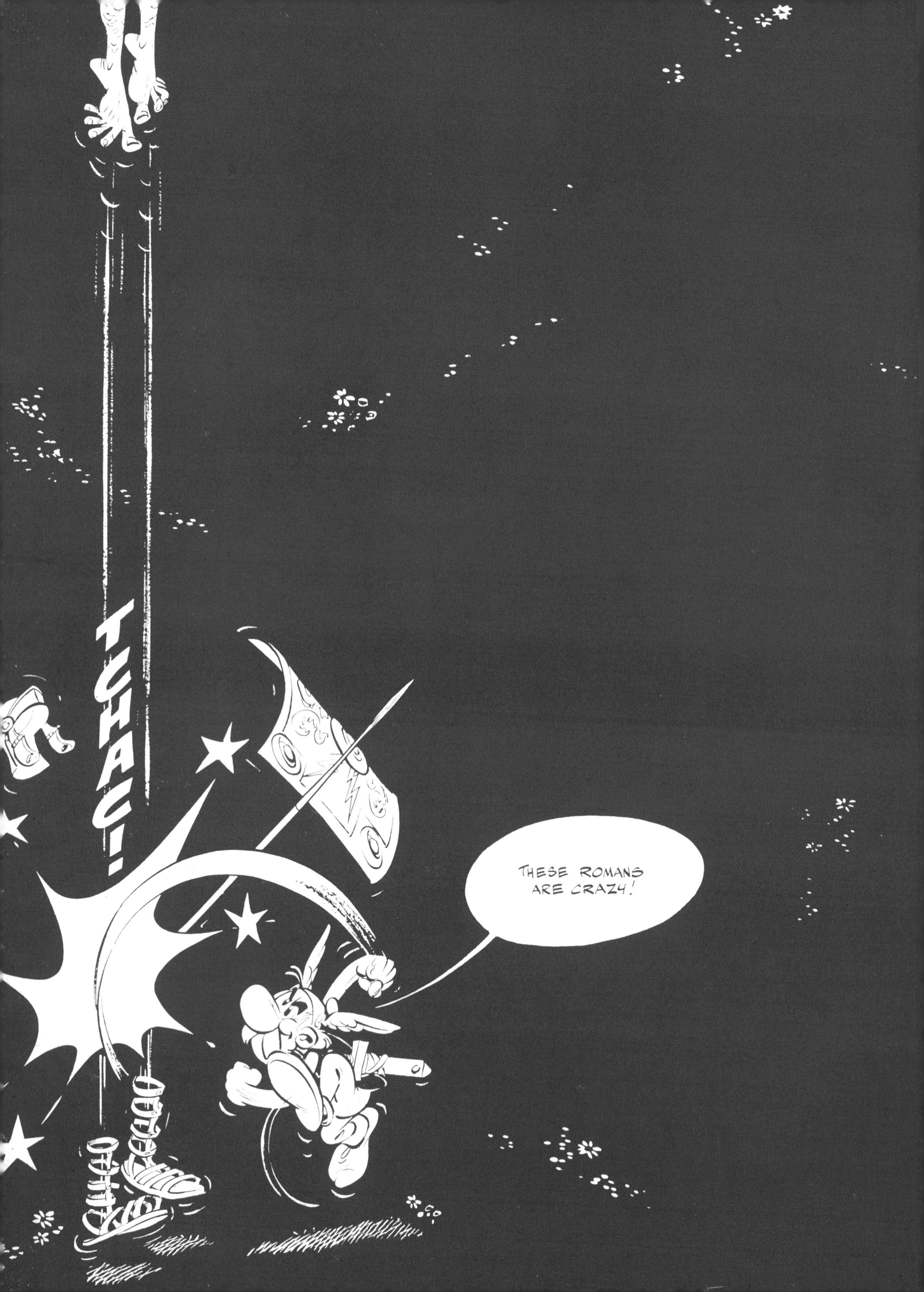
TCHAC!
THESE ROMANS ARE CRAZY!